This book belongs to

_____

_____

_____

For Elvira and Mel
C.M.

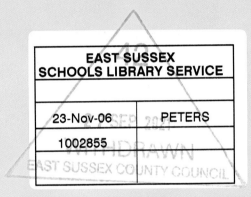
First published in 2005 in Great Britain by Gullane Children's Books
This paperback edition published in 2006 by
Gullane Children's Books

an imprint of Pinwheel Limited
Winchester House, 259-269 Old Marylebone Road,
London NW1 5XJ

1 3 5 7 9 10 8 6 4 2

Text and illustrations © Charlotte Middleton 2005

The right of Charlotte Middleton to be identified
as the author and illustrator of this work has been asserted by her
in accordance with the Copyright, Designs, and Patents Act, 1988.

A CIP record for this title is available from the British Library.

ISBN-13: 978-1-86233-610-0
ISBN-10: 1-86233-610-5

Printed and bound in Singapore

NOT OLD ENOUGH

Charlotte Middleton

GULLANE
CHILDREN'S BOOKS

It was almost
Eva's birthday.

But she was feeling fed up of being
the smallest and the youngest in her family.

She could NEVER reach the   biscuits . . .

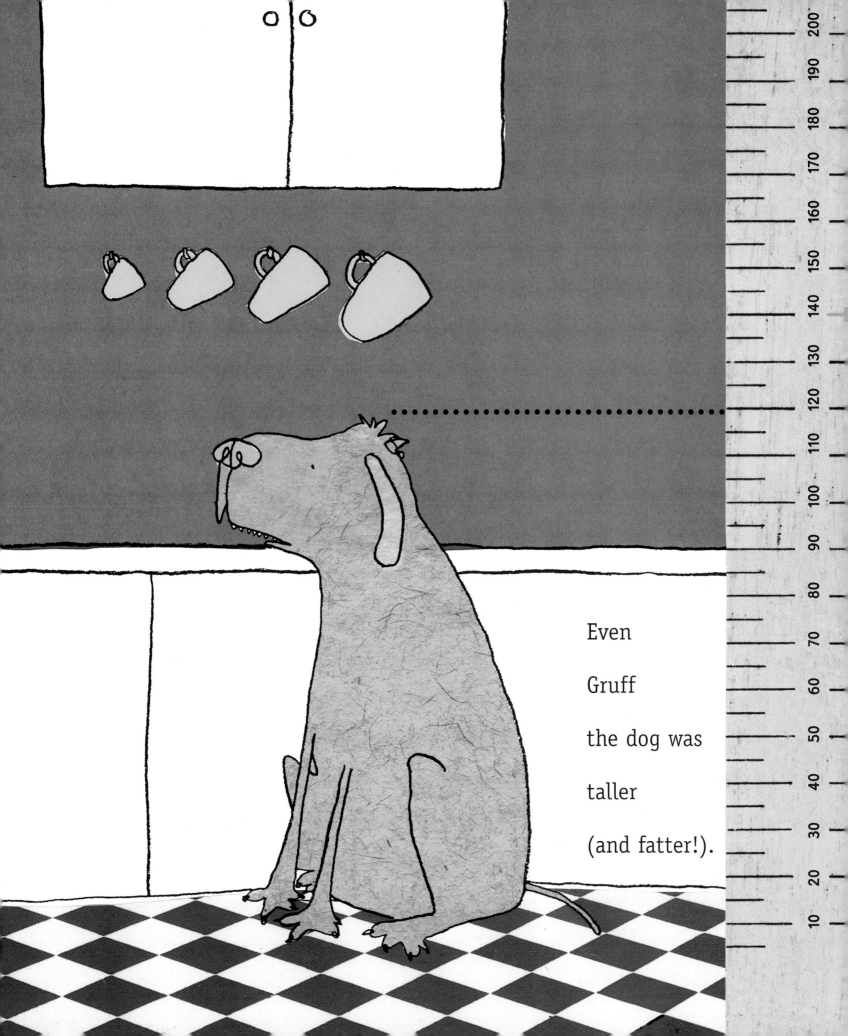

Even

Gruff

the dog was

taller

(and fatter!).

She always had to
stand in goal because
Billy said she was
too small to kick
the ball properly . . .

"Eva! Bedtime"

she *always*
had to go to bed
the earliest . . .

. . . and she wasn't allowed the pretty pink pointy shoes she'd seen in the shop.

Her mummy always said
"Sorry, Eva, you're just
not old enough . . ."

The day before her birthday,
Eva decided to put on her
mummy's things to make
herself look really grown up . . .

but Billy laughed
and said she looked

"absolutely
RIDICULOUS!"

. . . well, that was the final straw.

Eva decided she would
show her family that
she was old enough to
do whatever she wanted!
So she packed her things
and moved out . . .

to the *very* end
of the back garden!

She set up her own new home . . . (well, eventually!)

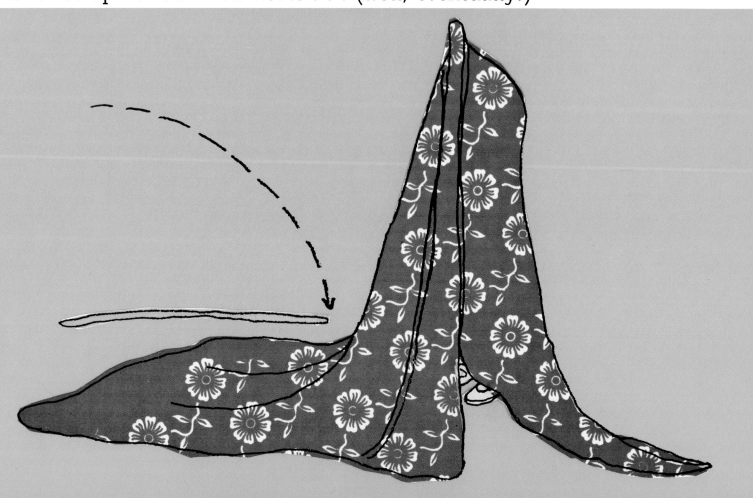

and she felt really **grown-up.**

She planned to get a job.
Probably as an **extremely famous**
clothes designer . . .

and she planned
to buy **pointy** shoes
and wear **bright pink** lipstick
and **everyone** would
admire her!

hottest
fashions!

After Eva had finished planning her
new grown-up life, it felt very late.
So she decided to go to bed.

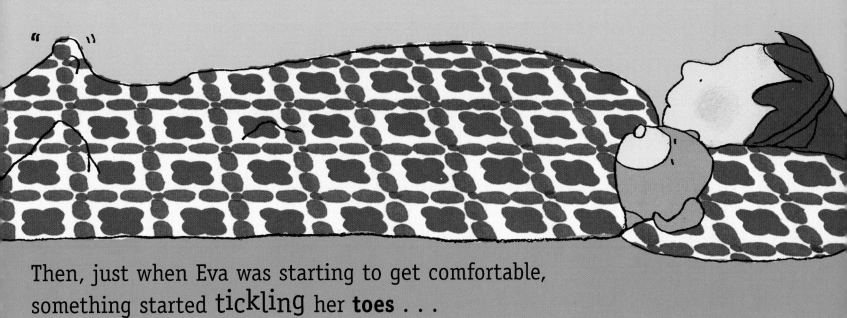

Then, just when Eva was starting to get comfortable,
something started tickling her toes . . .

and then it tickled her fingers . . .

and then . . .

Aaagh!

It was the
BIGGEST,
hairiest,
spider
in the whole *world* . . .

. . . **and** it was
on Eva's nose!

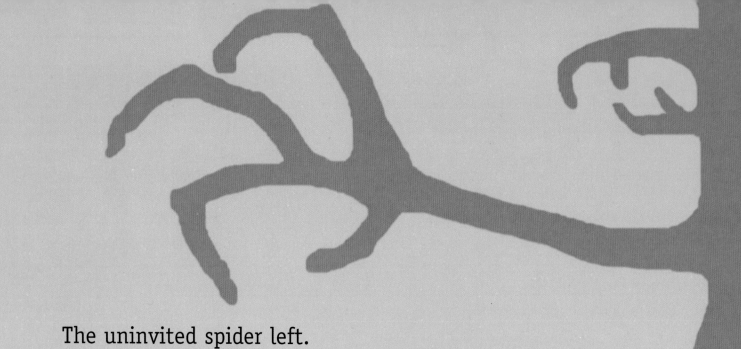

The uninvited spider left.
But before Eva had even had a chance to
close her eyes again, she saw a

HUGE monster standing outside!

Now that Eva was a grown-up
she felt she had no choice but to
have a stern word with the monster
(even though this would be very scary) . . .

Luckily, it wasn't a monster after all!

Eva felt really quite tired now, and a bit lonely. . .
and it was very hard to sleep

on two **bumpy** rocks
that wouldn't budge!

Being a grown-up was not so fun anymore.
And just when Eva's tummy was starting to
rumble ever so loudly, she heard something else . . .

There was a rustling
and a snuffling
sound . . . and it
was getting closer

and closer!

It was Gruff and Billy!
Eva had to admit – she was more than a tiny bit pleased to see them.
"There you are!" said Billy. "Please come back to the house for supper –
we've been worried about you!"

Eva was really glad that Billy and Gruff had come to find her!
Perhaps, she thought, *being the youngest isn't so bad after all . . .*

And for her birthday the next day,
Eva got the best present EVER from
Mummy and Billy . . .

It was a new pair of **pink, sparkly** shoes (with bows)!!
Eva **loved** them! They made her feel grown-up,
and **very special** indeed.

Other Gullane Children's Books
for you to enjoy . . .

The Star Who Fell Out of the Sky

Ian Robson • Ian Newsham

New Kid In Town

Claire Freedman •
Kristina Stephenson

Big Yang and Little Yin

Angela McAllister • Eleanor Taylor